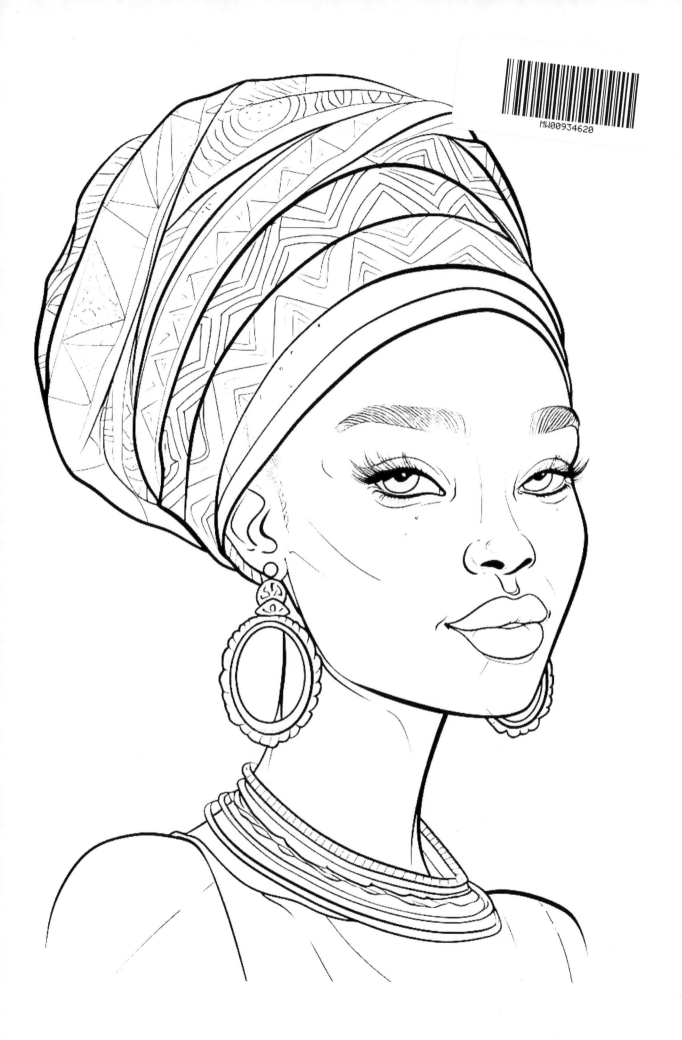

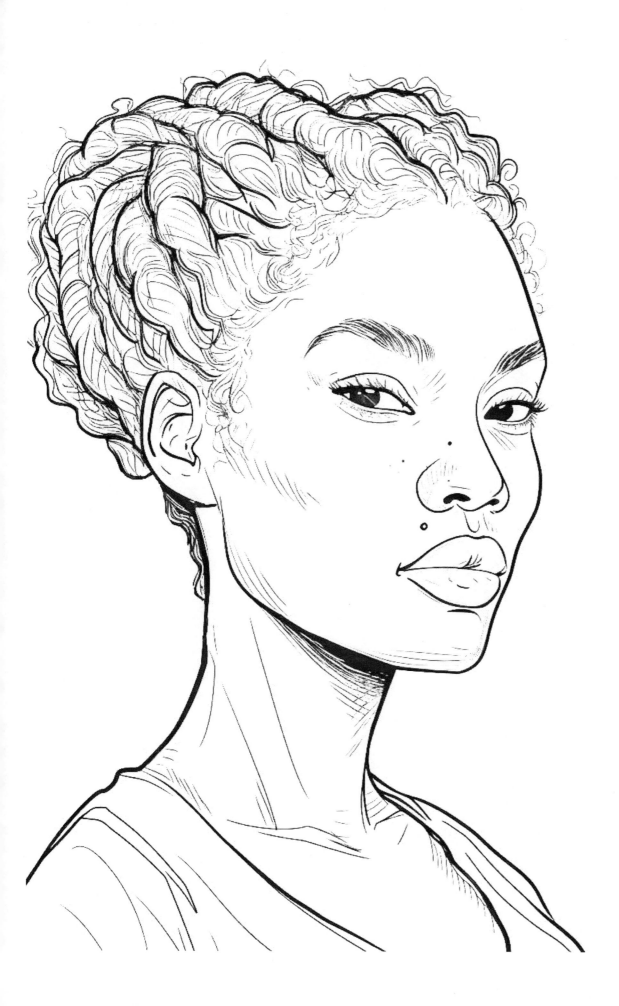

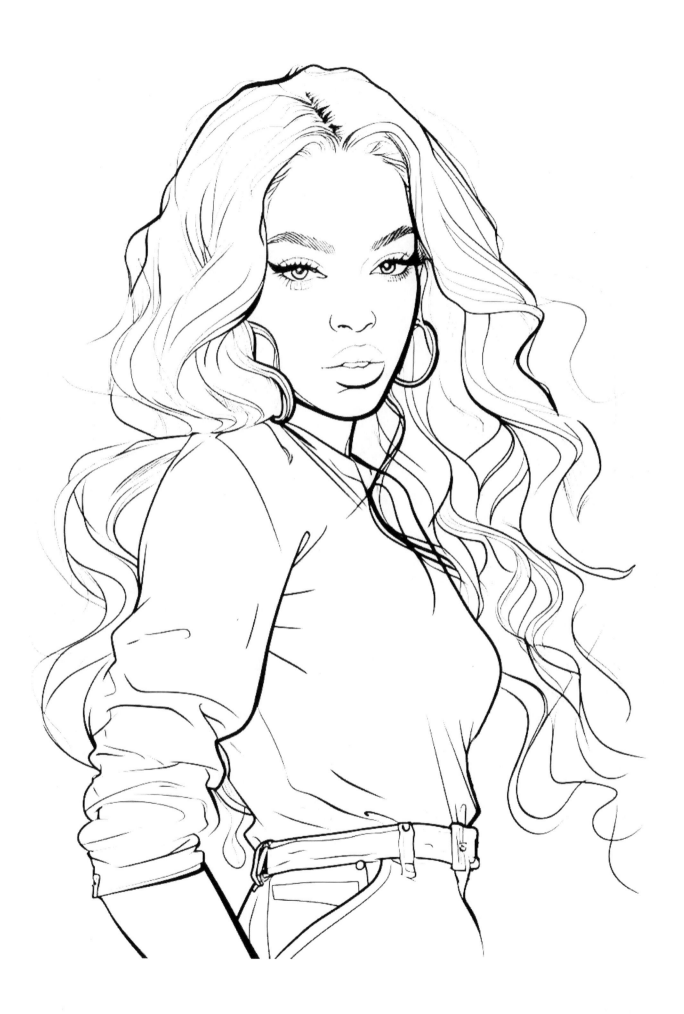

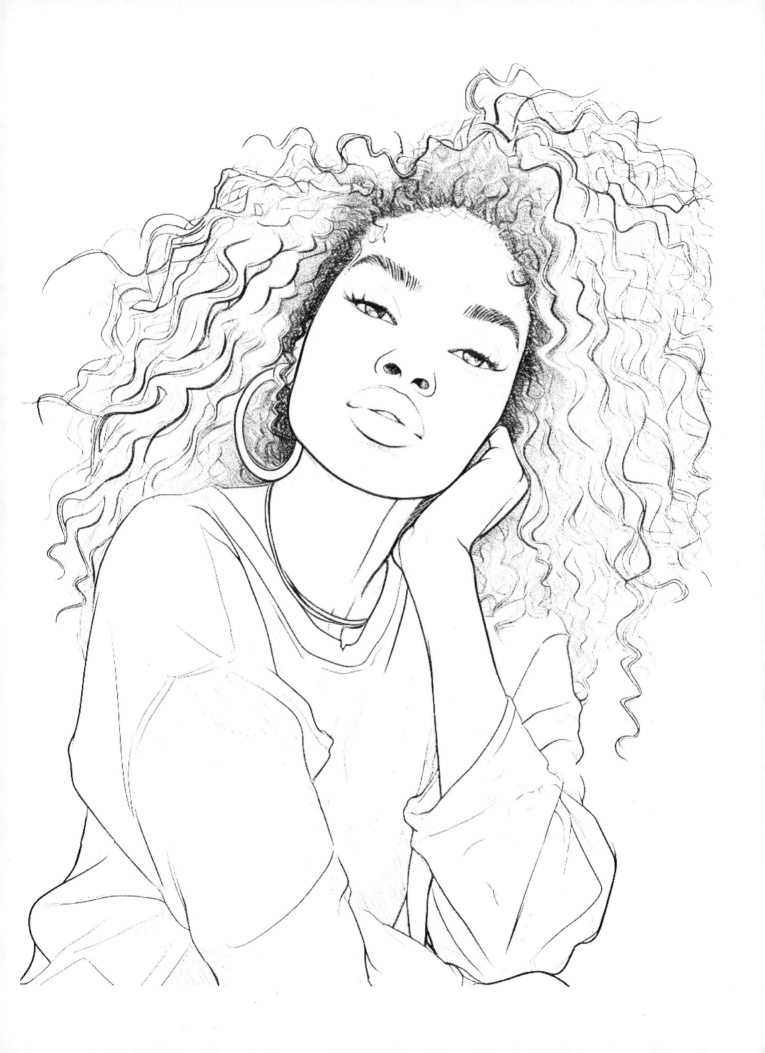

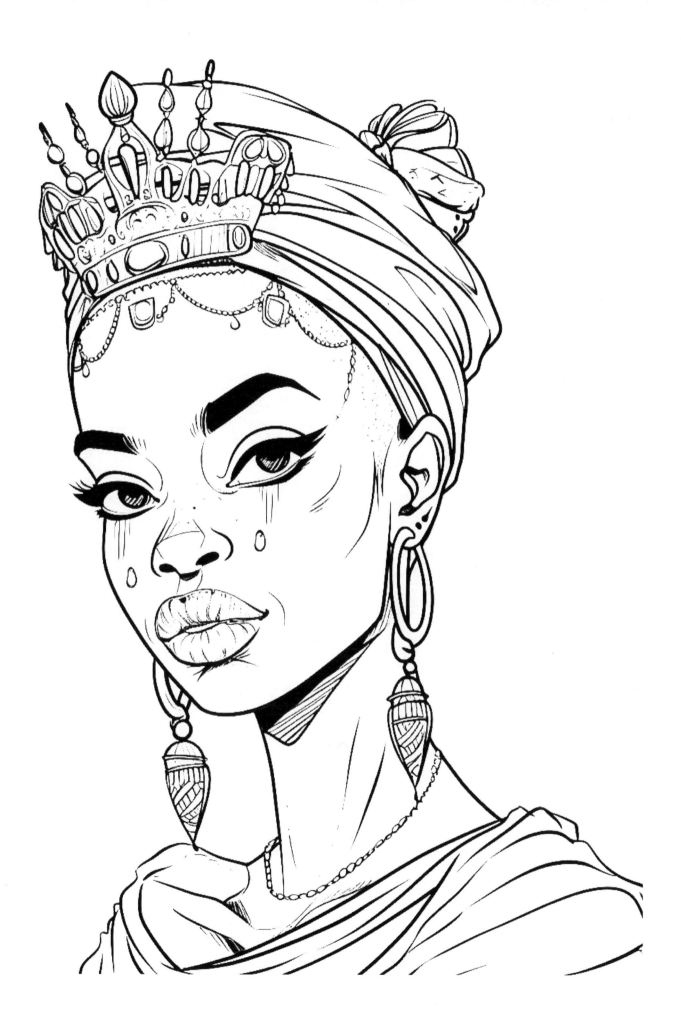

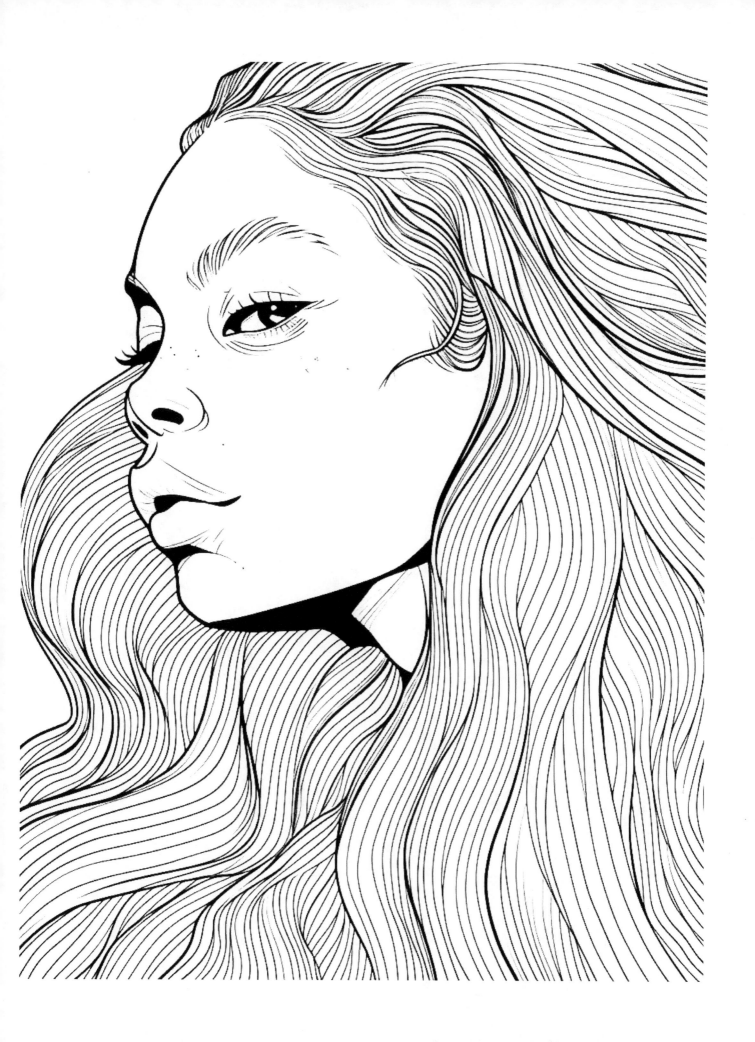

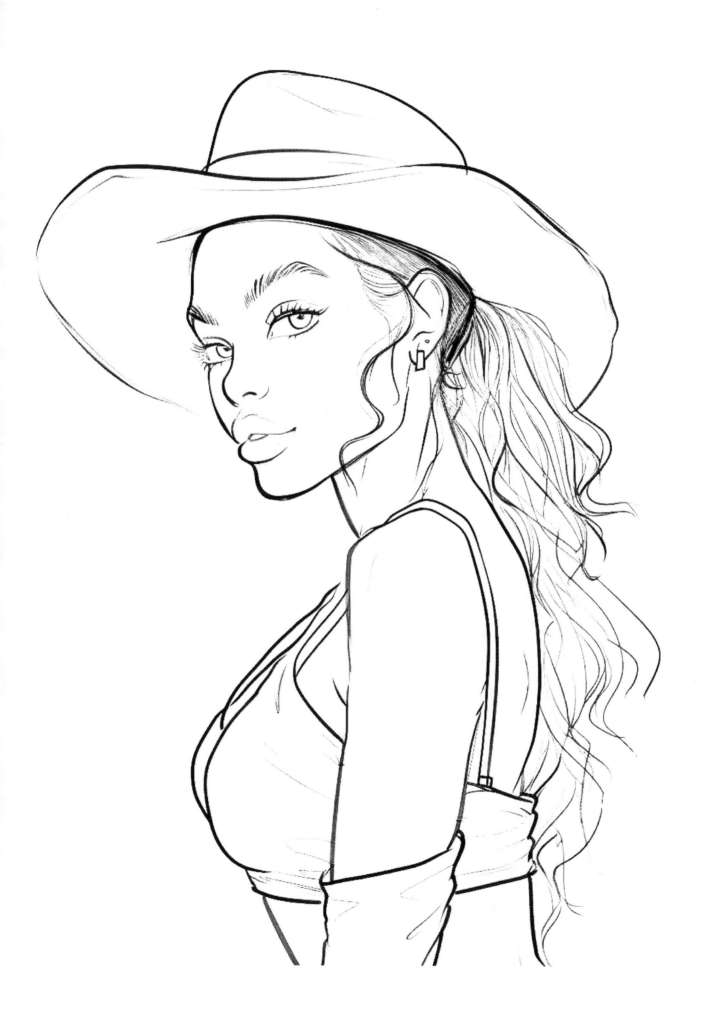

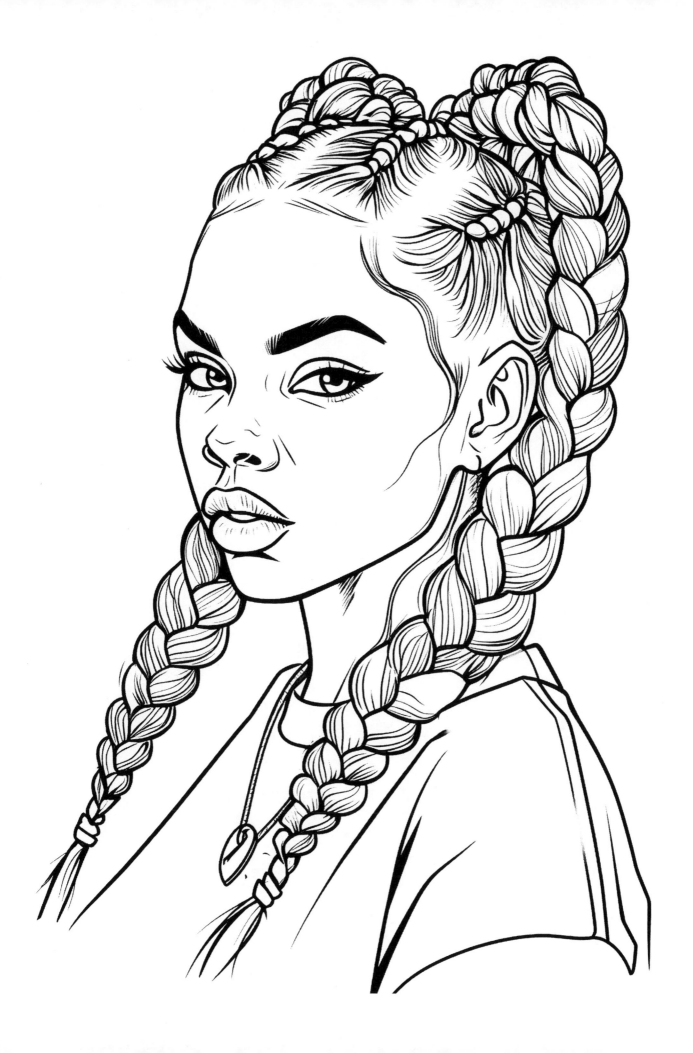

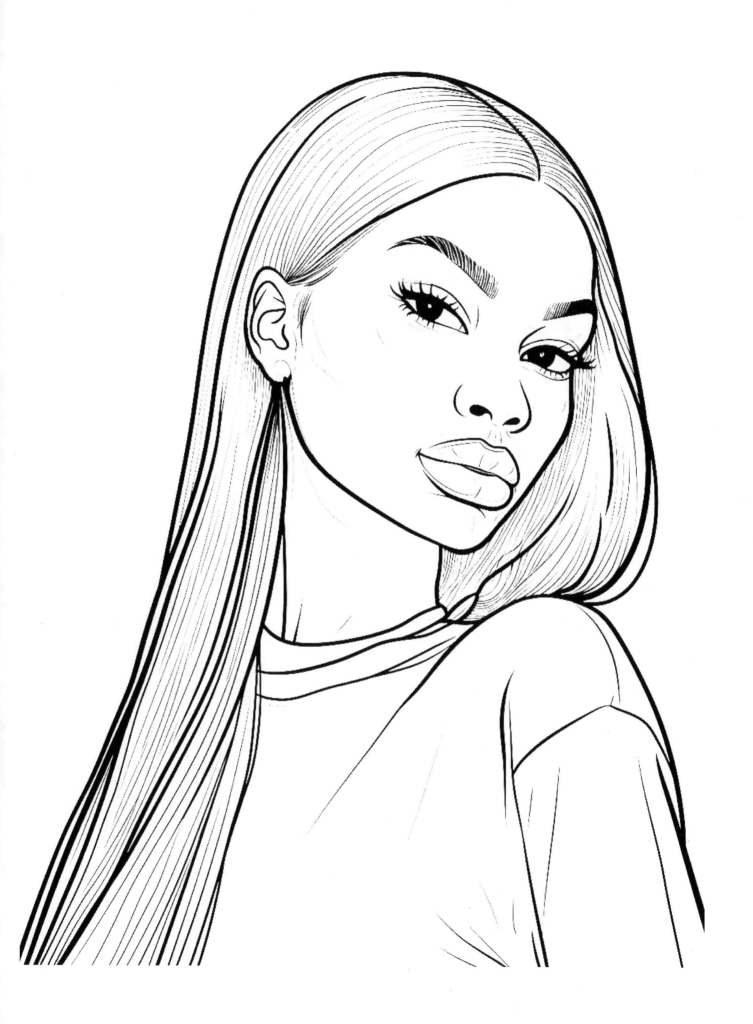

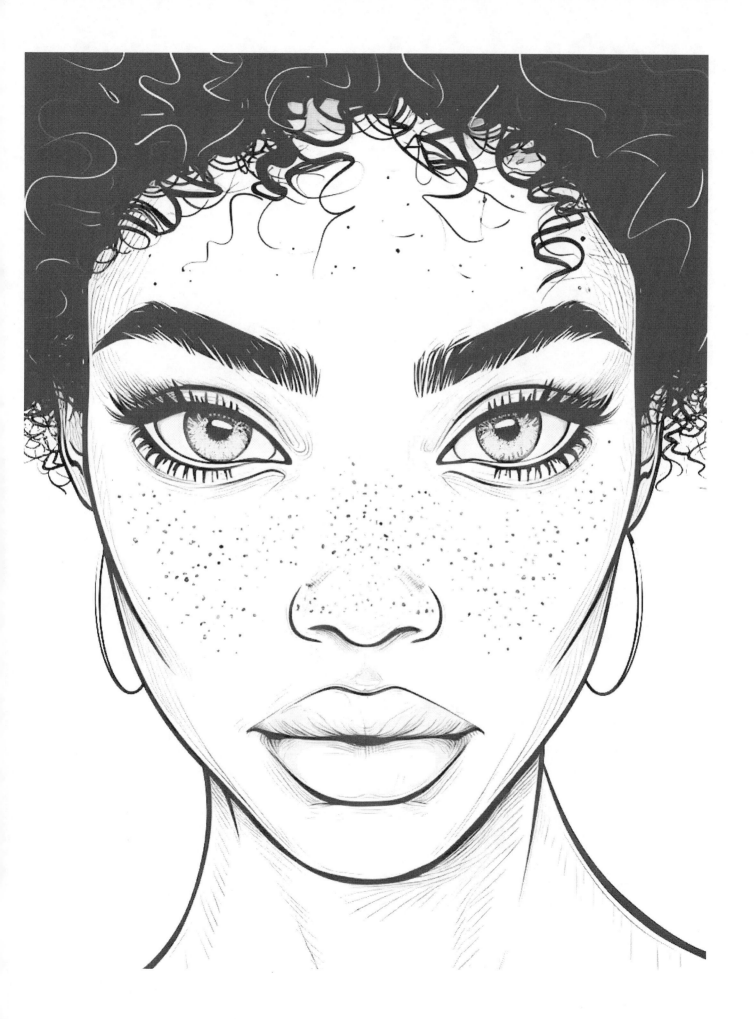

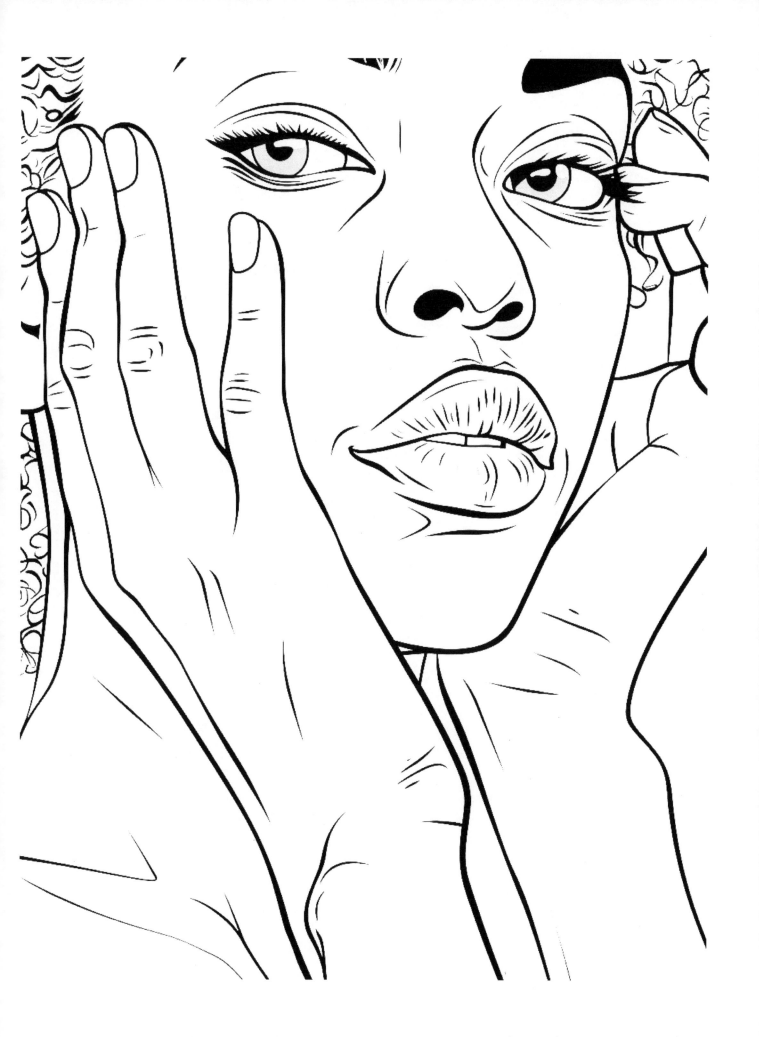

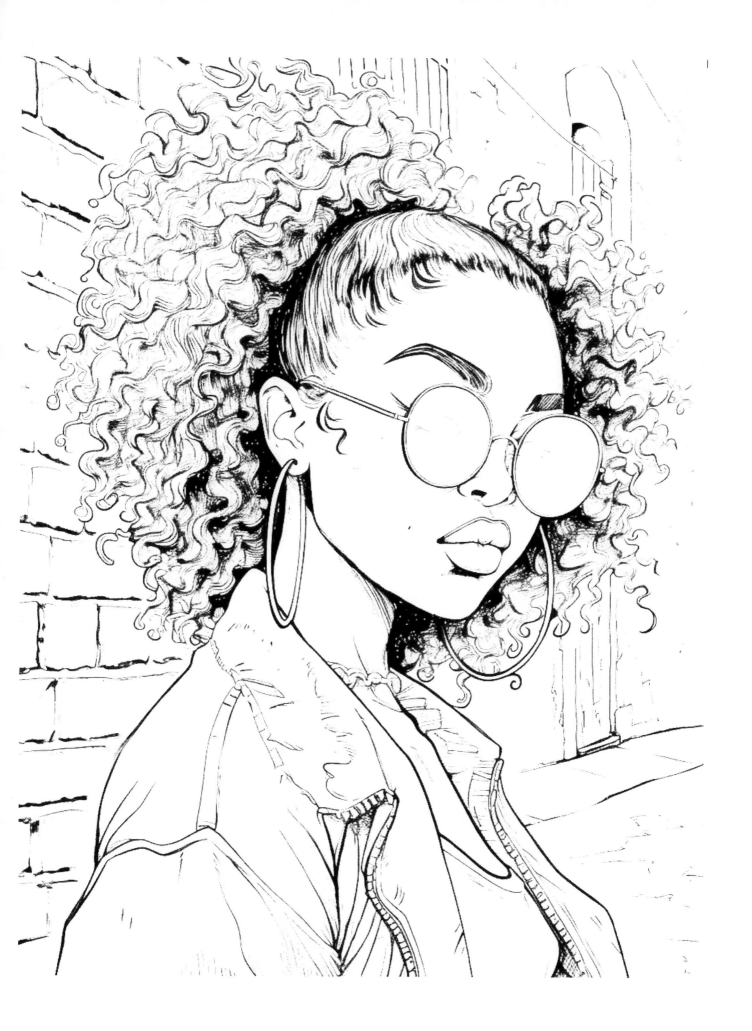

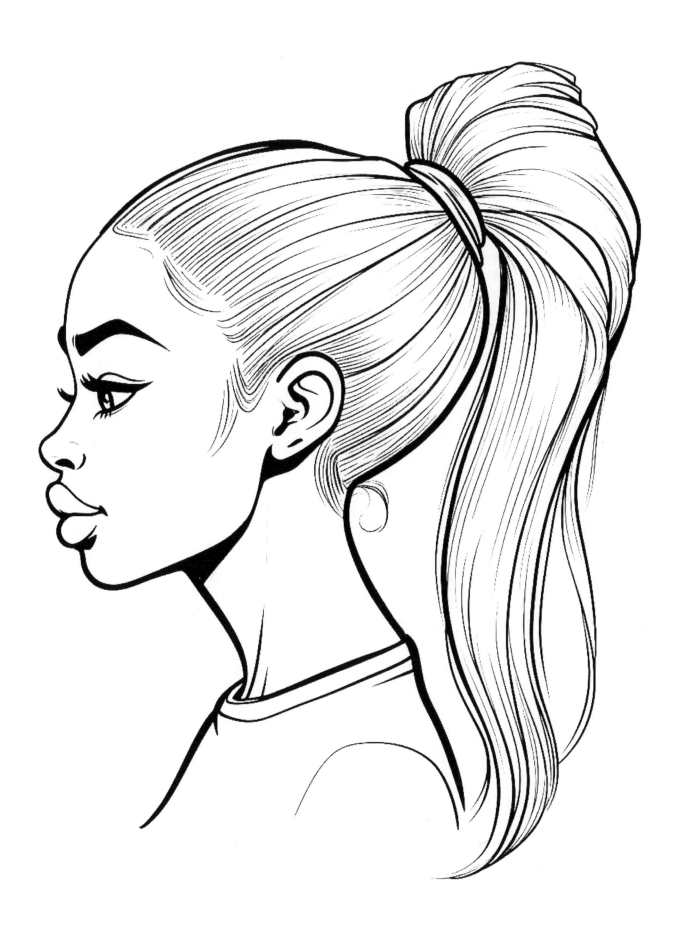

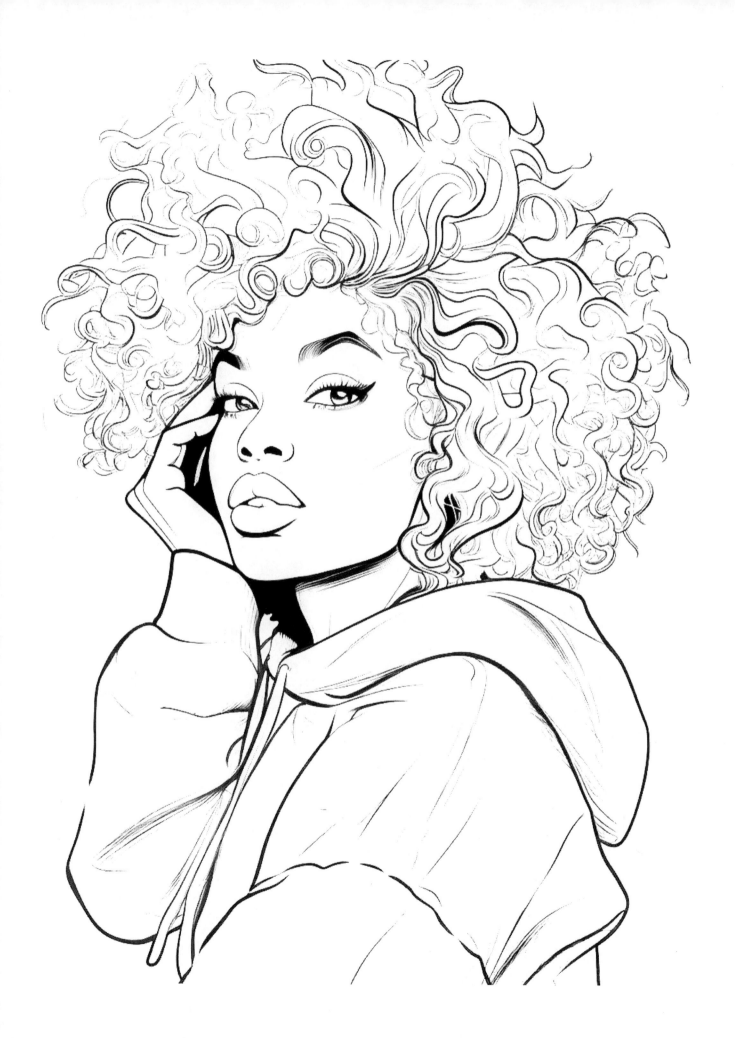

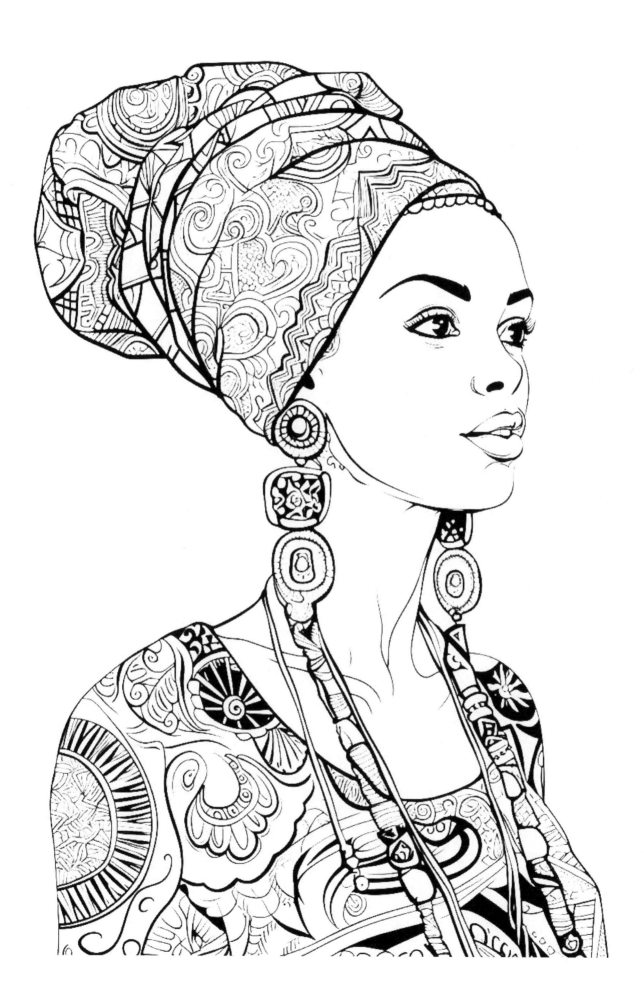

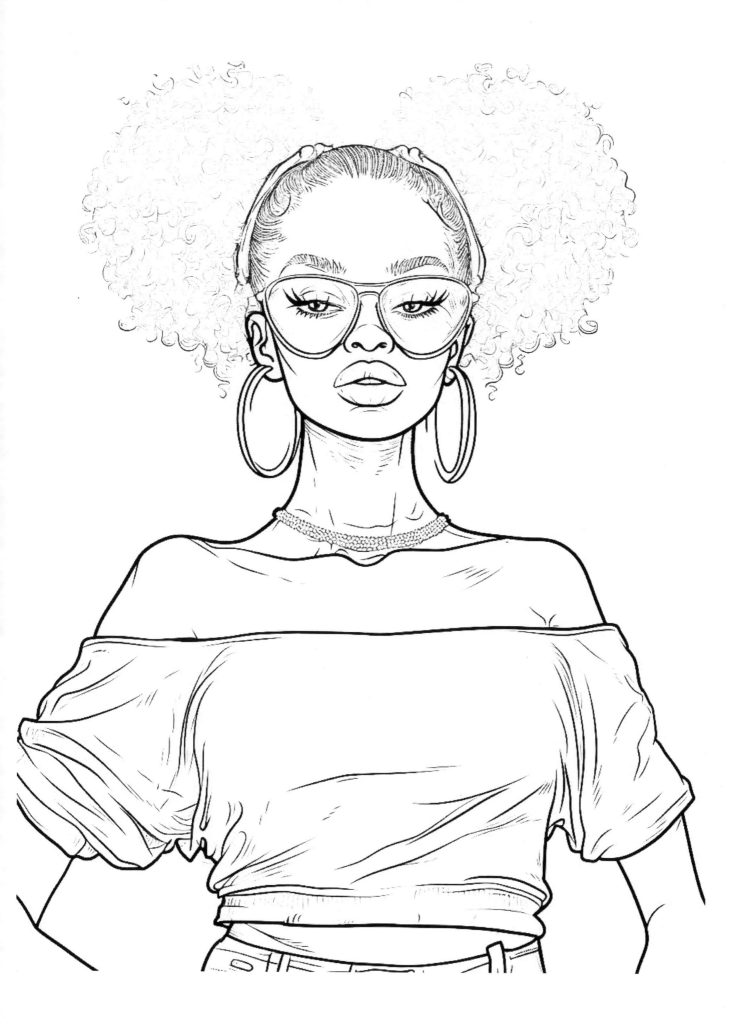

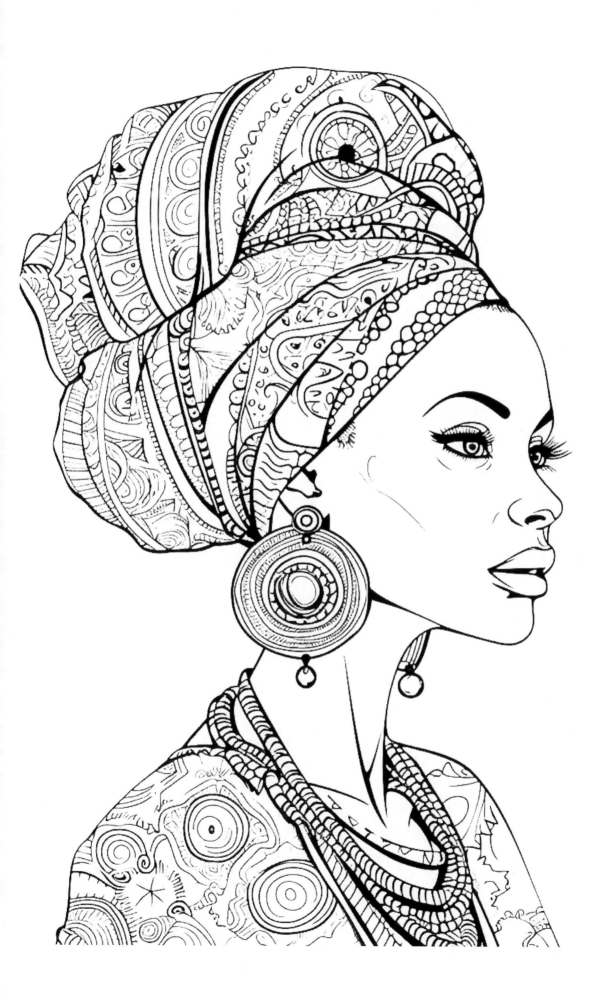

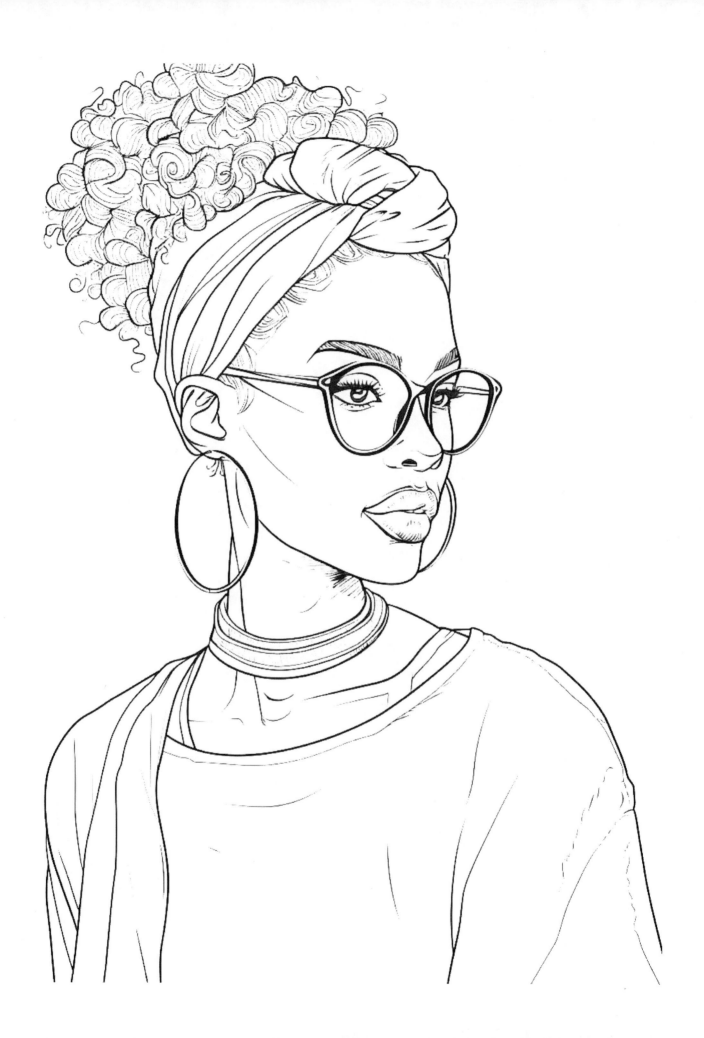

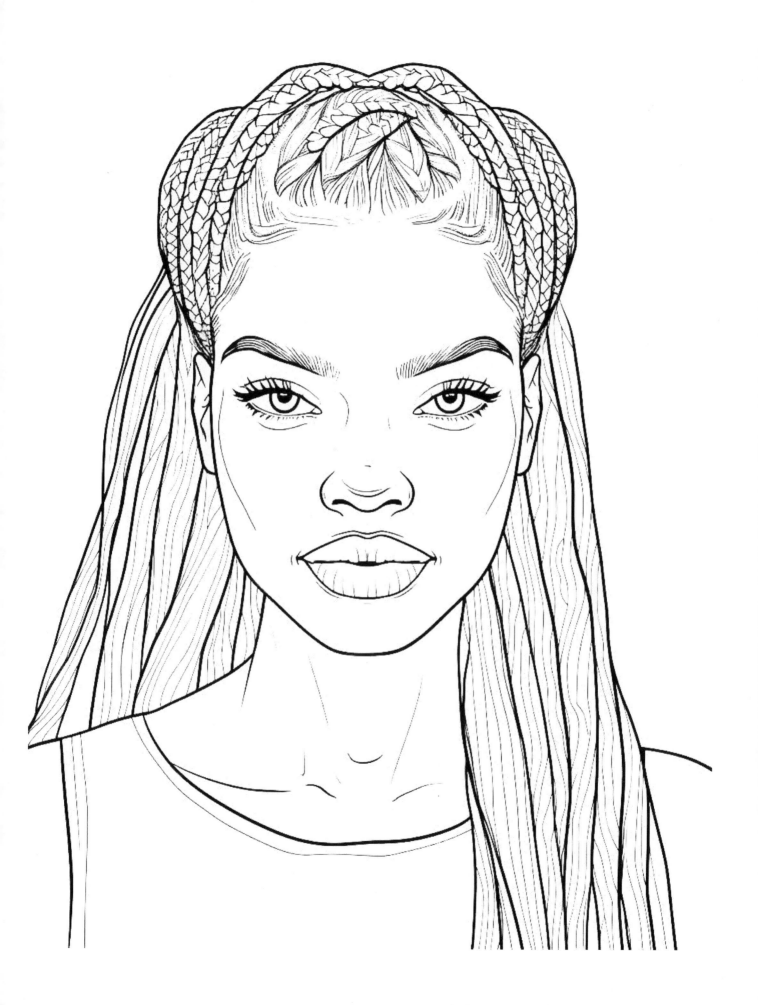

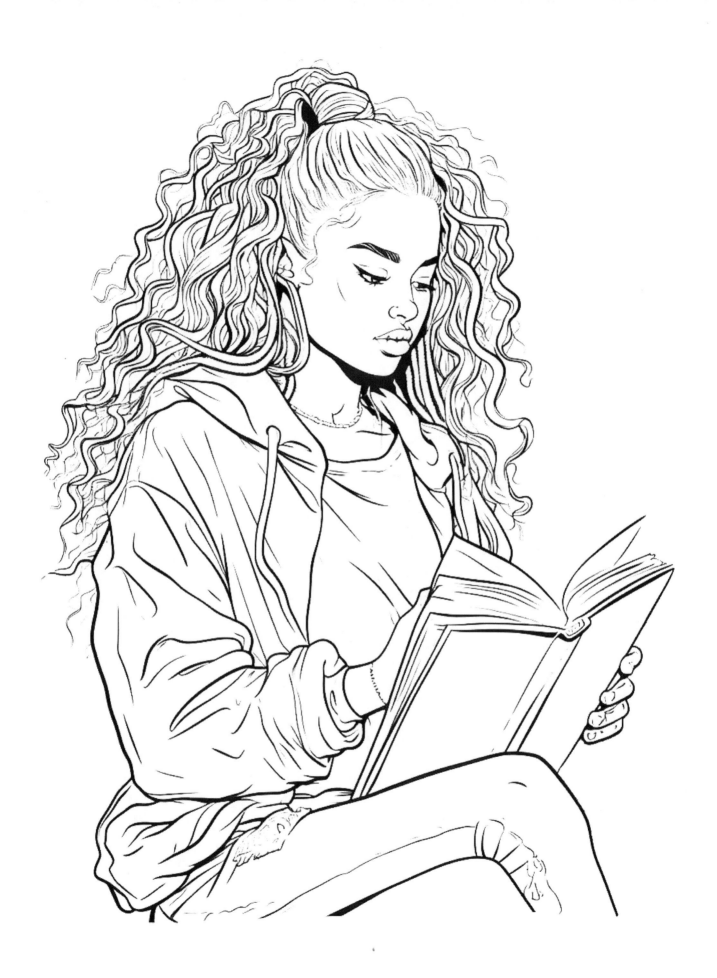

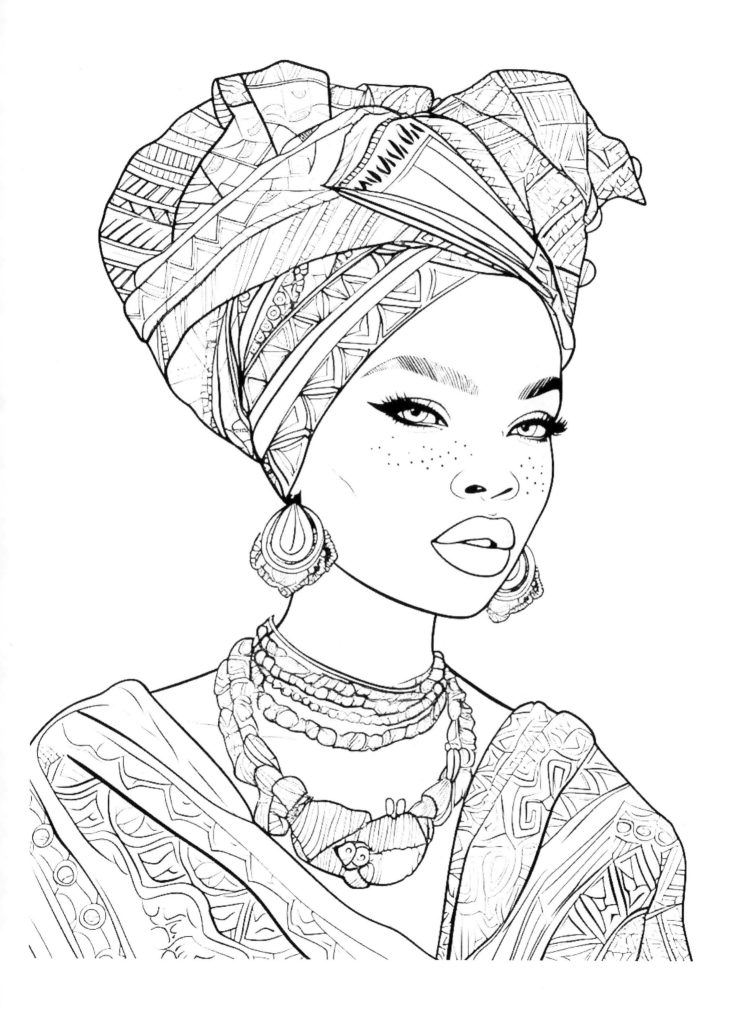

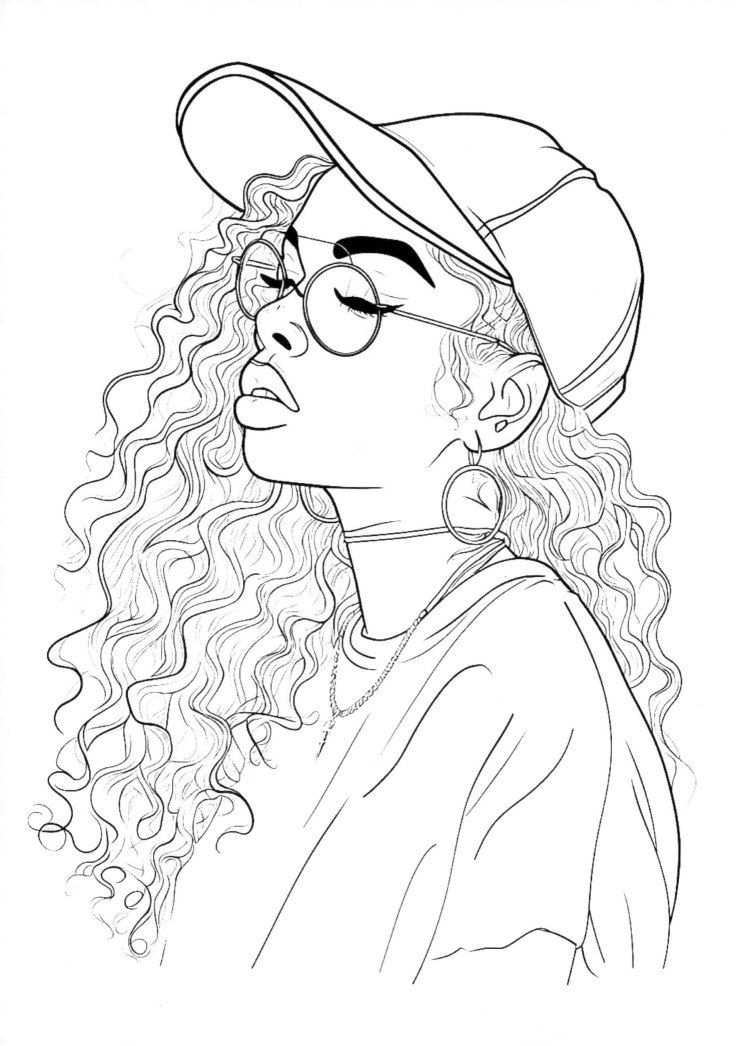

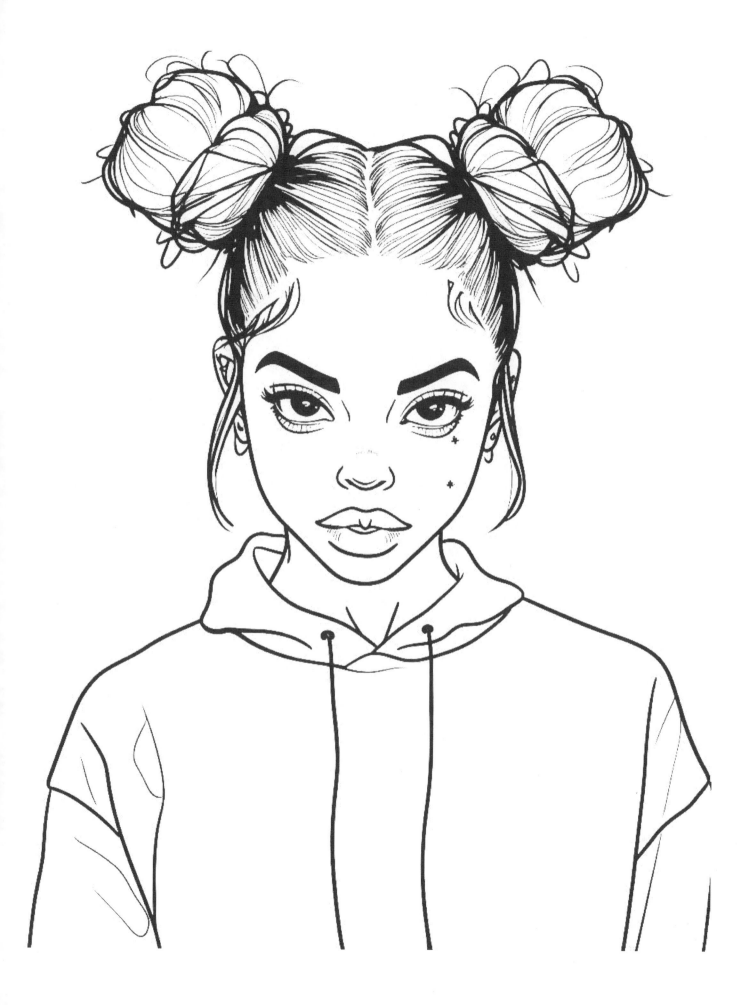

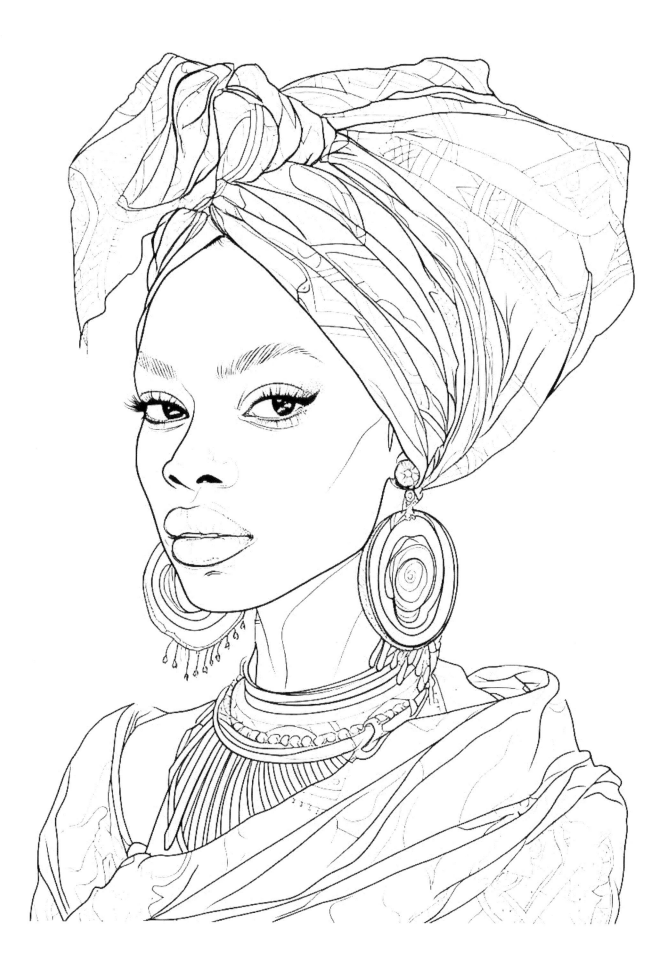

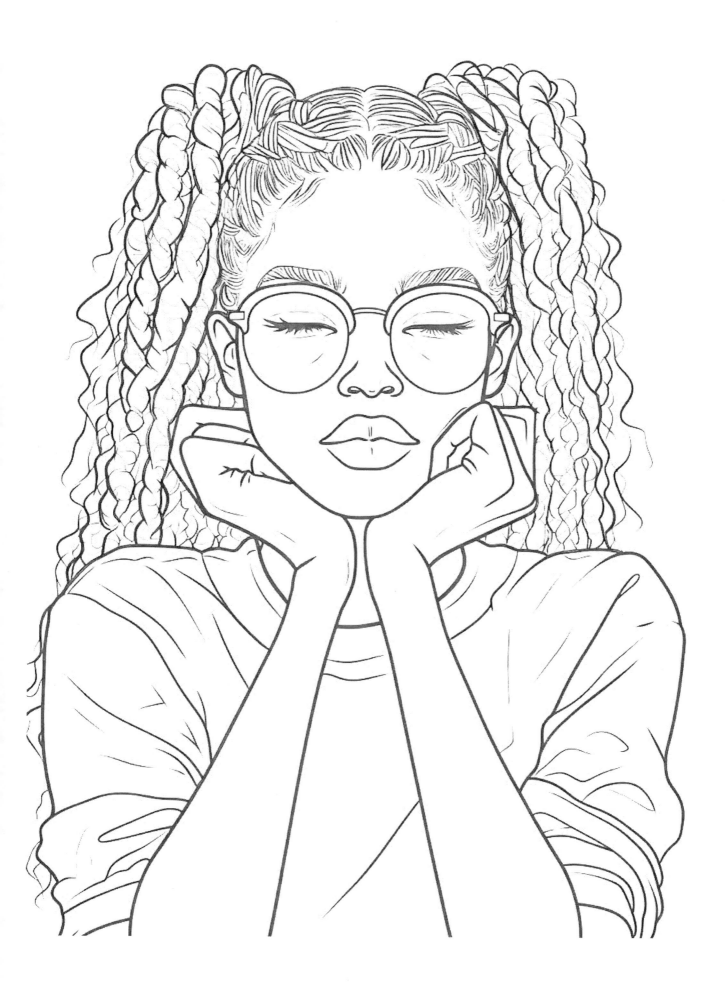

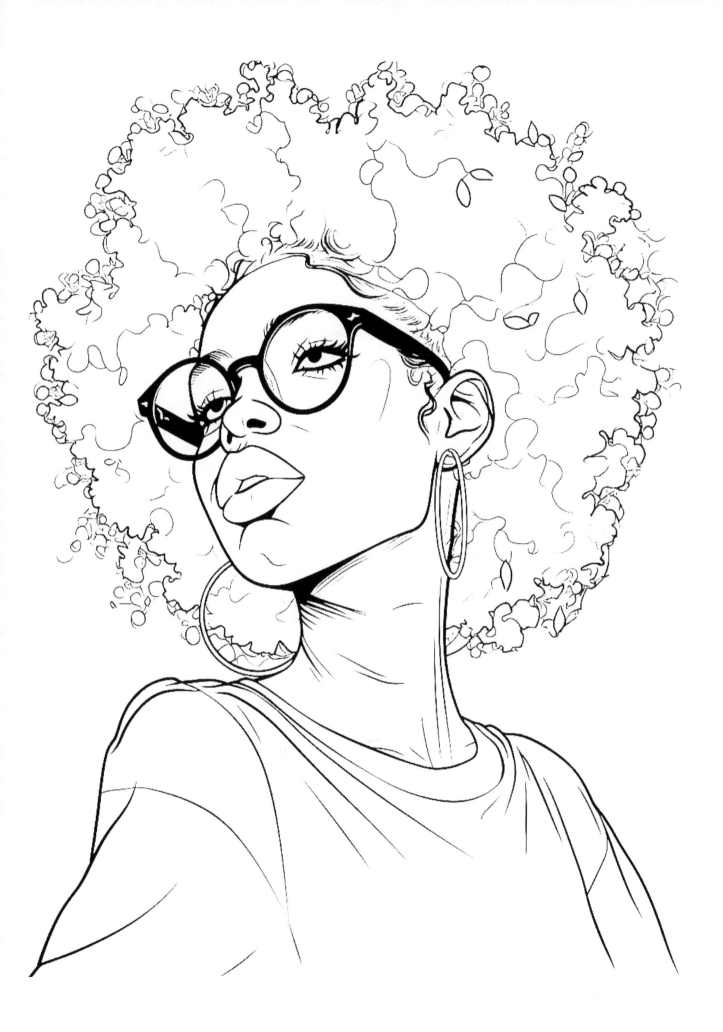

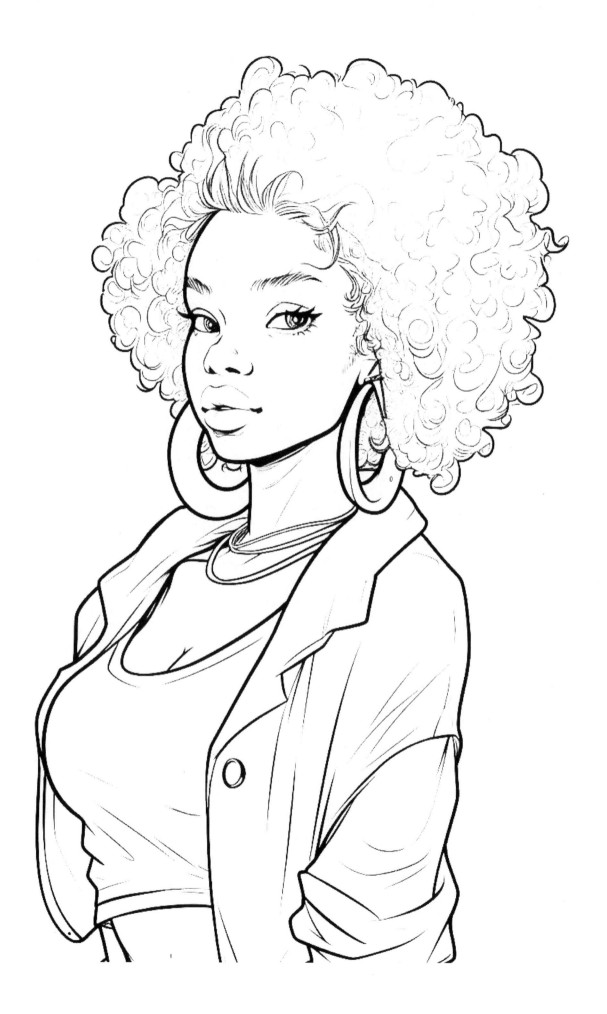

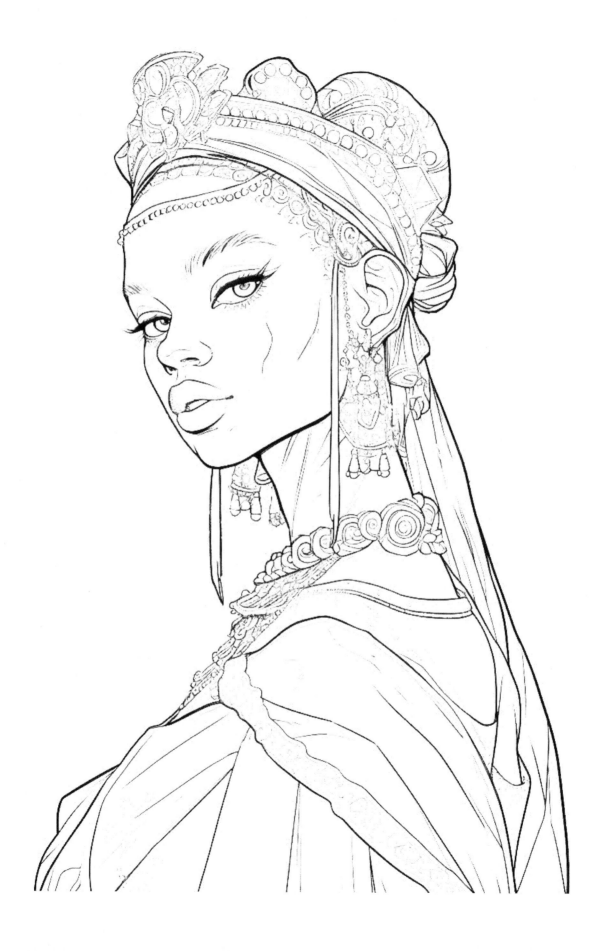

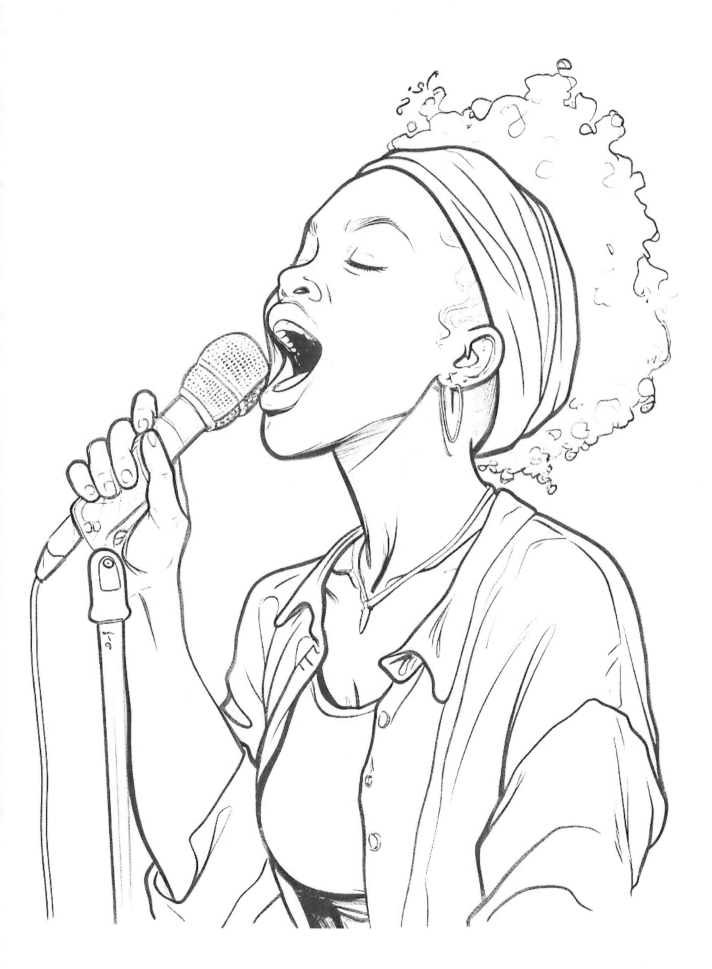

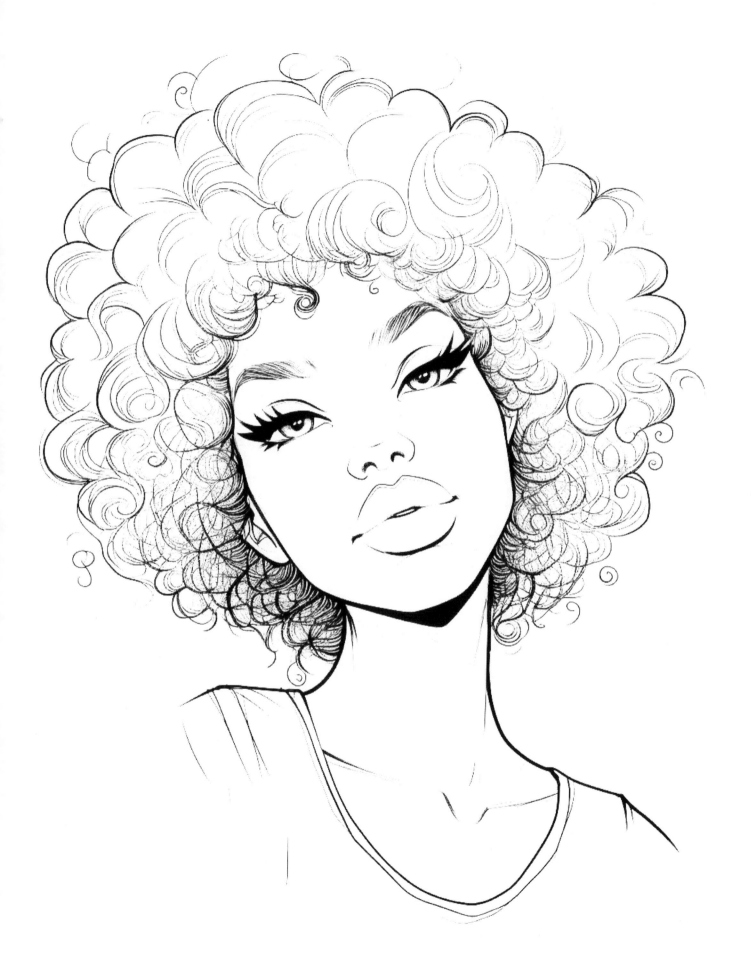

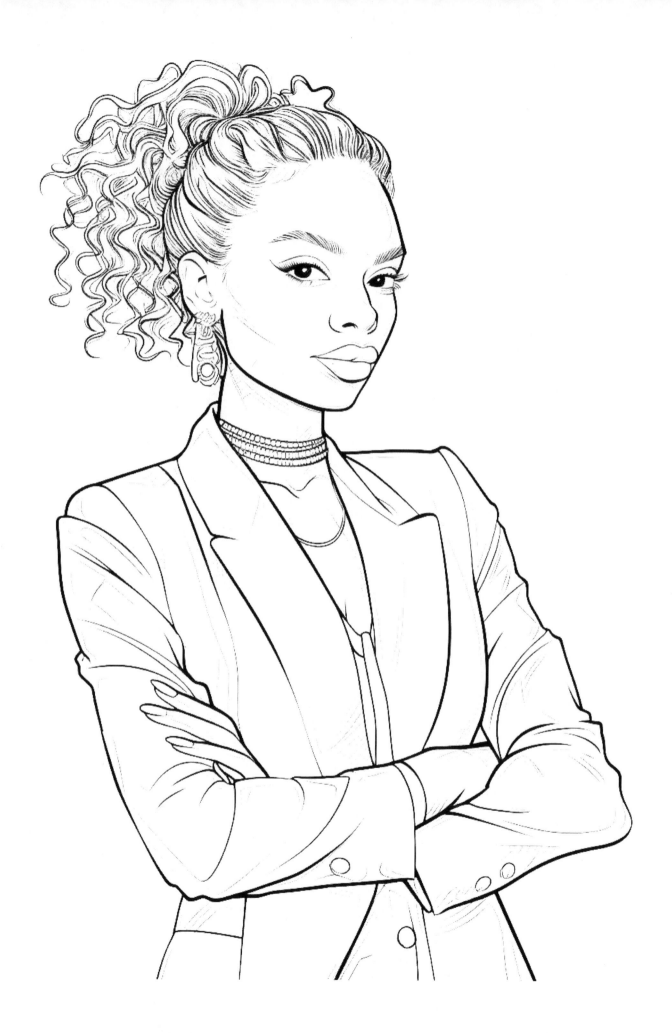

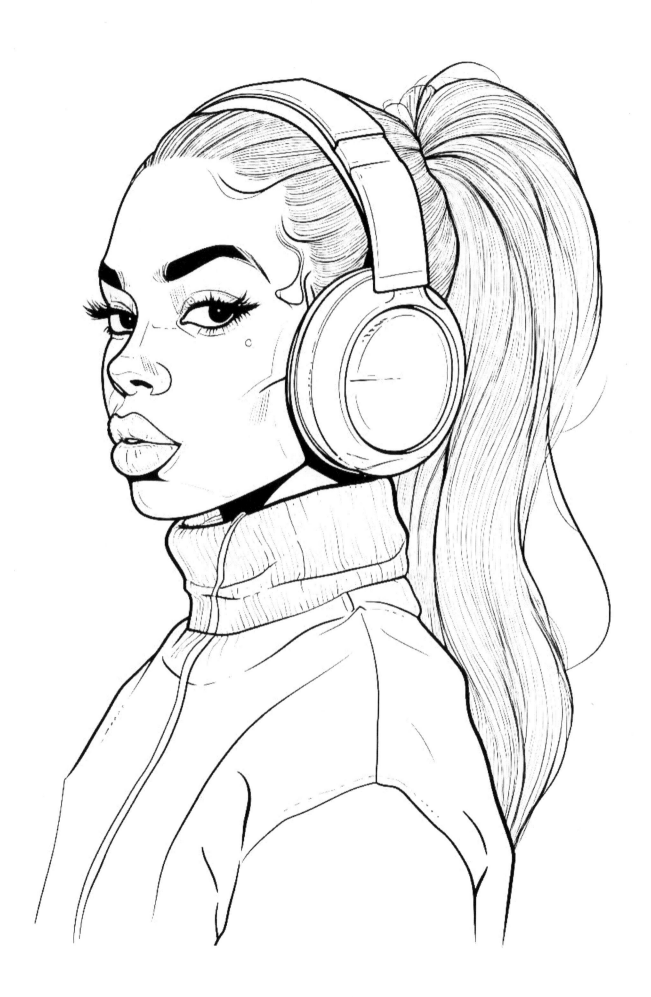

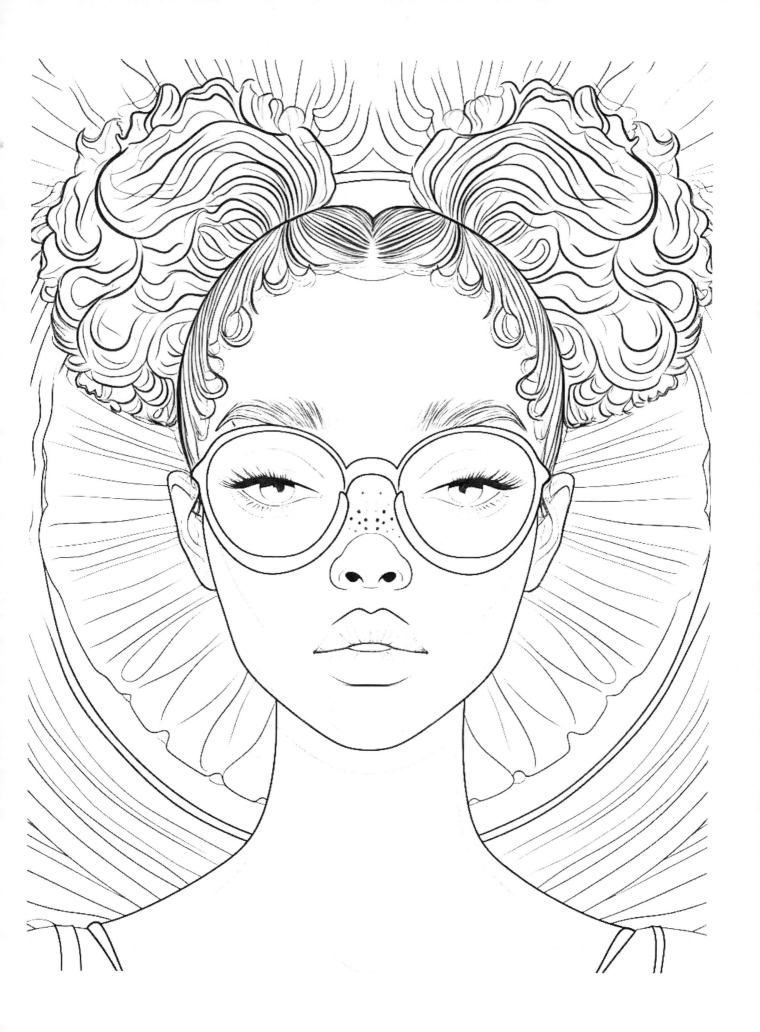

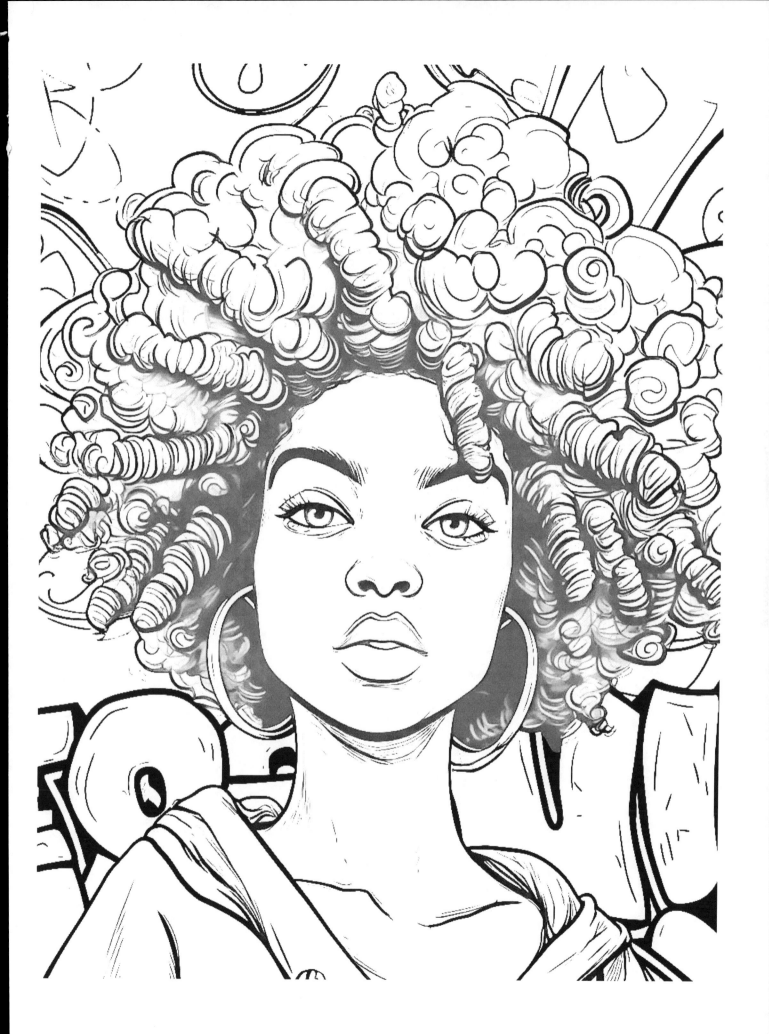

Thank you for choosing our coloring book to add a splash of creativity to your life! We appreciate your trust in our product and hope it brings you endless joy and inspiration.

Cassandra Lynne

Made in the USA
Monee, IL
10 December 2024

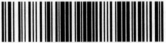